The Wheels on the

illustrated by Annie Kubler

go round and round

Child's Play (International) Ltd
Ashworth Rd, Bridgemead, Swindon, SN5 7YD UK
Swindon   Auburn ME   Sydney
© 2001 Child's Play (International) Ltd Printed in Heshan, China
ISBN 978-0-85953-136-8   HH2905138X807131368
17 19 20 18
www.childs-play.com

The wheels on the bus go Round and Round,
Round and Round, Round and Round.

The wheels on the bus go Round and Round, All day long!

Round and Round

The wipers on the bus go Swish Swish Swish,
Swish Swish Swish, Swish Swish Swish.